can

They Can Be Best Friends

by Liza Charlesworth

ISBN: 978-1-338-78280-6
Illustrated by Chester Bentley
Copyright © 2021 by Liza Charlesworth. All rights reserved.
Published by Scholastic Inc., 557 Broadway, New York, NY 10012

10 9 8 7 6 5 4 3 2 1   68   21 22 23 24 25 26 27/0

Printed in Jiaxing, China. First printing, June 2021.

Can a chair and a bear
be best friends?
Yes, they **can**!

Can a spoon and a moon
be best friends?
Yes, they **can**!

3

Can a mouse and a house
be best friends?
Yes, they **can**!

Can a crown and a clown
be best friends?
Yes, they **can**!

Can a pail and a snail
be best friends?
Yes, they **can**!

Can a bee and a three
be best friends?
Yes, they **can**!

Can a boy and a toy
be best friends?
Yes, they **can**!